Rose in the River

Ann Thwaite

Illustrated by John Dyke

 CHILDRENS PRESS, CHICAGO

For Alice, whose adventure it was.

Library of Congress Cataloging in Publication Data

Thwaite, Ann.
  Rose in the river.

  SUMMARY: Rose goes on an outing with her family and
has an adventure in the river.
  I. Dyke, John, 1935-   II. Title.
PZ7.T43Ro3   [E]   75-40348
ISBN 0-516-03589-4

American edition published 1976 by
Regensteiner Publishing Enterprises, Inc.
All rights reserved. Printed in the U.S.A.
Published simultaneously in Canada.

First published 1974 by Knight books and
Brockhampton Press Ltd, Salisbury Road, Leicester
Printed in Great Britain by Cox & Wyman Ltd,
London, Fakenham and Reading
Text copyright © 1974 Ann Thwaite
Illustrations copyright © 1974 Brockhampton Press Ltd

Rose was out for the day. So were Rose's Mom, Rose's Dad, Rose's Grandma, Rose's Grandpa and Bill. Bill was Rose's dog.

It was a hot day.

Rose was hot. "I feel like a popsicle," said Rose.

"You don't look like one, Rosie," said Grandpa."

"*Rose*," said Rose.

"*Rose*," said Rose's Mom.

"It's time we stopped," said Rose's
Mom. "Look for somewhere to stop,
Dad."

"This looks like a nice place," said Grandpa.

"Smelly," said Mom.

"Flies," said Grandma.

"Cows," said Rose.

Bill put his head out of the window
and barked.

Dad drove on.

"This looks like a nice place," said
Grandma.

"No shade," said Mom.

"Burrs," said Grandpa.

"Buttercups," said Rose.

Bill put his head out of the window and barked.

Dad drove on.

"This looks like a nice place," said
Rose.

"We can have some tea," said Mom.

"I'd like that," said Grandma.

"It's time we stopped," said Dad.
Grandpa opened the door. Rose and
Bill jumped out.

Rose had a popsicle.

Mom had a nice cup of tea.

So did Dad and Grandma and Grandpa.

Bill had a bowl of water.

Rose took off her dress. She had her swimsuit underneath.

Dad blew up her rubber ring.

"Nice place for a swim," Mom said.

Grandpa and Grandma went to sleep.
So did Bill.
Mom and Dad and Rose went into
the river.

"It's cold," said Mom.

"Nice," said Rose.

There were lots of people in the river.
They shouted and splashed in the water.
It was a shallow river. It was too
shallow for anyone big to swim. The
water came up to Dad's knees.

It was deep enough for Rose to swim.

"Look at me," she shouted. "Look at me, I'm swimming."

"Look at Rose," Mom shouted. "She's swimming and she's going!"

Dad and Mom tried to run after Rose. But the sharp stones and the water slowed them down.

Rose was going faster and faster.
"Look at me! Look how fast I'm
swimming!"

The people in the river were shouting, "Help! Look at the child!" They tried to run in the water.

The people on the riverbank were shouting, "Help! Look at the child!" They ran along the riverbank.

Bill woke up and ran, too.

Rose was going farther and farther away. The swift current carried her along. There was a bend in the river. Rose was getting nearer and nearer the bend.

There was a man fishing in the river. He heard the shouting people. He heard Bill bark. He saw Rose. He fished her out of the river.

Then he walked up the river in his big boots. He gave Rose back to her Mom.

"I swam faster than a fish," Rose said.
"I nearly drowned."